Jean M. Cooper

Illustrated by Pamela Stanley

My Name is

ALEX

the Keeper of the Gate

WestBow Press books may be ordered through booksellers or by contacting:

WestBow Press
A Division of Thomas Nelson & Zondervan
1663 Liberty Drive
Bloomington, IN 47403
www.westbowpress.com
844-714-3454

Because of the dynamic nature of the Internet, any web addresses or links contained in this book may have changed since publication and may no longer be valid. The views expressed in this work are solely those of the author and do not necessarily reflect the views of the publisher, and the publisher hereby disclaims any responsibility for them.

Any people depicted in stock imagery provided by Getty Images are models, and such images are being used for illustrative purposes only.
Certain stock imagery © Getty Images.

Illustrated by Pamela Stanley.

Scripture taken from the New King James Version®. Copyright © 1982 by Thomas Nelson. Used by permission. All rights reserved.

ISBN: 978-1-6642-4836-6 (sc)
ISBN: 978-1-6642-4837-3 (e)

Library of Congress Control Number: 2021922137

Print information available on the last page.

WestBow Press rev. date: 11/10/2021

WestBow
PRESS®
A DIVISION OF THOMAS NELSON
& ZONDERVAN

This book is dedicated to support the education program for the Roma Gypsy children in Romania. It is my hope that it will bring awareness and help combat the social injustice and prejudices that have plagued these people for centuries. All of the proceeds from this book will support the education of Roma and Romanian children. That they may learn to love one another despite their differences under the Cross of Christ. To in turn become all God has called them to be. For more info contact www.beliefinmotion.org.

Hello, my name is Alex. I am a Roma Gypsy who lives in the city of Sibiu in Romania. I am a Gate Keeper, with no special job or calling in my daily life.

I'm just Alex, the keeper of the gate.

I come to the gate daily and watch the people come and go through the city. No one ever sees me, but I watch them. I see how they are all in such a hurry to go to work and to school. But no one ever notices me at all.

I am Alex, the keeper of the gate.

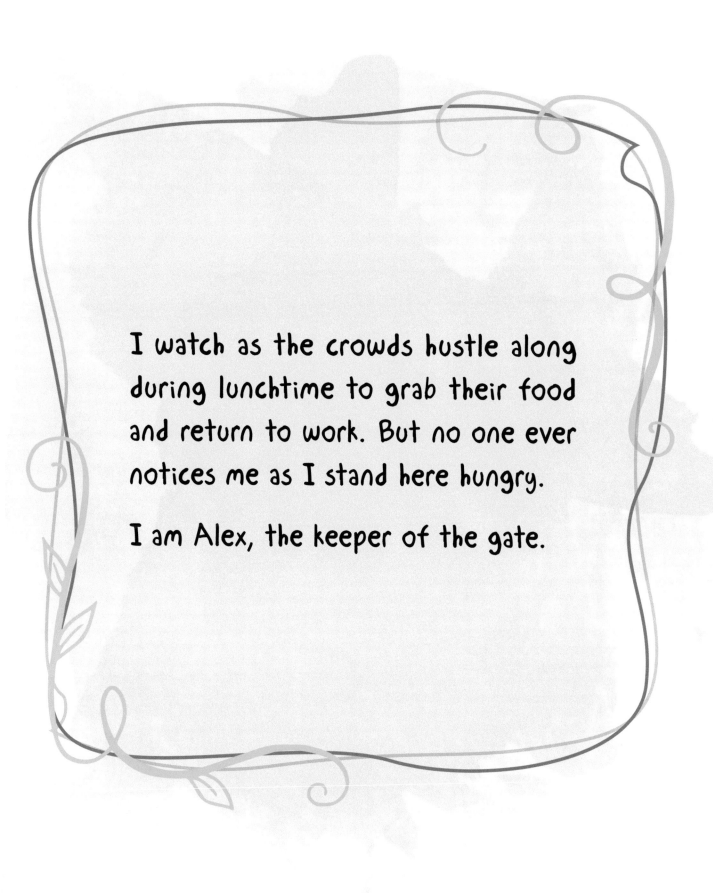

I watch as the crowds hustle along during lunchtime to grab their food and return to work. But no one ever notices me as I stand here hungry.

I am Alex, the keeper of the gate.

As the sun goes down, I watch men, woman and children rush along the path of the gate to return to their warm homes and prepare hot meals for their families.

I am Alex, the keeper of the gate.

I stand by as the keeper of the gate, hoping that someone will give me a glance, and just maybe, see what God sees: that I am hungry and cold, and that I'd like to go to school and learn to read and write. I too have dreams and hopes, but no one knows them.

I am Alex, the keeper of the gate.

You see, I am not the only Gate Keeper. There are many of us throughout the city, but no one notices us until three white vans drive through the gate. The vans actually stop, and the people inside ask my name. I smile and tell them,

"My name is Alex, the keeper of the gate."

They respond that they are missionaries who have come to the city on God's behalf to bring good news to all who will listen. They give me bread, treats, socks, and a pair of boots.

I am Alex, the keeper of the gate.

I am so excited that someone notices me, and I tell them so. They ask if I know of anyone else who needs help in Sibiu. "Yes," I say, "we are the Gate Keepers. We are all over the city, but no one saw us until you came."

I am Alex, the keeper of the gate.

The missionaries sit down and explain that they are here to spread the good news: that God so loved the world that He sent His only Son Jesus to save us, and whoever would believe in Him would have eternal life. (John 3:16)

The missionaries also tell me that children like me are the Gate Keepers of God's important Kingdom, and that we hold the keys to the future of Sibiu and Romania. I am Alex, the keeper of the gate.

The missionaries gather me and the other Gate Keepers from the city with their vans. They feed us and clothe us. They teach us how to read and write so we can learn the Bible, and we do. We all grow in wisdom and stature.

I am Alex, the keeper of the gate.

How grateful we all are that someone paid attention to us! I am still Alex, the keeper of the gate, but I no longer live a beggar's life, watching the world pass me by. Our missionary friends cared for us as Jesus would have. They taught us through their actions that we can have faith in a God who cares for us through the hearts and hands of people.

I am Alex, the keeper of the gate.

Now, I too have eyes filled with God, and I look for other Gate Keepers. I show them the same love that I was given myself, and greet them by saying, "Hello, my name is Alex, the keeper of the gate."

Printed in the United States
by Baker & Taylor Publisher Services